FIX-IT

# FIX-IT

by David McPhail

E. P. Dutton · New York

for Ann, who helped



*Library of Congress Cataloging in Publication Data*
McPhail, David M.
Fix-it.
Summary: It is when the fix-it man is trying to repair the television and her parents are trying to entertain her that Emma becomes so interested in reading, she no longer cares about TV.
[1. Television—Fiction.
2. Books and reading—Fiction] I. Title.
PZ7.M2427Fi 1984 [E] 83-16459
ISBN 0-525-44093-3

Published in the United States by
E. P. Dutton, a division of
Penguin Books USA Inc.
Published simultaneously in Canada by
Fitzhenry & Whiteside Limited, Toronto

Editor: Ann Durell Designer: Isabel Warren-Lynch

Printed in Hong Kong by South China Printing Co.
10 9 8 7 W

One morning Emma got up early
to watch television.

But the TV didn't work.

Emma asked her mother to fix it.

"Hurry, Mom!" she cried.

Emma's mother tried to fix it.

But she couldn't.

Emma's father tried.

But he couldn't fix it, either.

So he called the fix-it man. “Please hurry,” he said. “It’s an emergency!”

The fix-it man came right away.

He tried to fix the TV. Emma's mother
and father tried to fix Emma.

Her father blew up a balloon…

until it popped.

Her mother sang a song.

So did the cat.

Her father pretended to be a horse—
but Emma didn't feel like riding.

Finally her mother read her a book.

"Read it again," said Emma when her mother had finished.

"And again."

"And again."

"Now *I'll* read to Millie," said Emma.
And she went to her room.

Then her father found out what was
wrong with the TV.

"I fixed it!" he called.

But Emma didn't come out of her room.

She was too busy.